Said a Flea to his dog . . .

"It's not you –
it is **me**!
Can't you see that this
flea simply *needs* to be
FREE?

"Free to see other dogs.

Free to
hop.

Free to
r o a m.

I'm hoping to find
A **new dog** for my home!

Too **tall**.

Too **short**.

"Too **loud**

and too **cheeky**.

Too frequently leaky.

"Too **busy**.

Too **calm**.

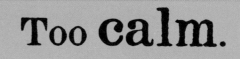

Too **city**.

Too **farm**.

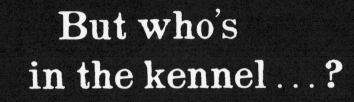

But who's
in the kennel ...?

"It's *hard* to find **perfect**.
I've searched day and night.

For Gaia, Aster and little Jonty – W.M.
For Thomas X – N.R.

HODDER CHILDREN'S BOOKS
First published in Great Britain in 2021
by Hodder and Stoughton

A CIP catalogue record
for this book is available
from the British Library.

HB ISBN: 978 1 444 95077 9
PB ISBN: 978 1 444 95078 6

10 9 8 7 6 5 4 3 2 1

Printed and bound in China

Hodder Children's Books,
an imprint of Hachette
Children's Group,
part of Hodder and Stoughton
Carmelite House,
50 Victoria Embankment,
London, EC4Y 0DZ
An Hachette UK Company
www.hachette.co.uk
www.hachettechildrens.co.uk

MIX
Paper from
responsible sources
FSC® C104740

Hodder
Children's
Books